WRITTEN BY RODNEY E. FREEMAN

ILLUSTRATED BY EDUARDO PAJ

First Published - 2022 This edition was published 2022 by Preservation Media LLC,
Charlotte,
LCCN: 2022917452

Ebook ISBN: 978-1-7367320-5-2

Little RODNEY the Librarian

Written by Rodney E. Freeman JR.
Illustrated by Eduardo Paj

**To my son always tell your own story
and look to God as your point of reference.**

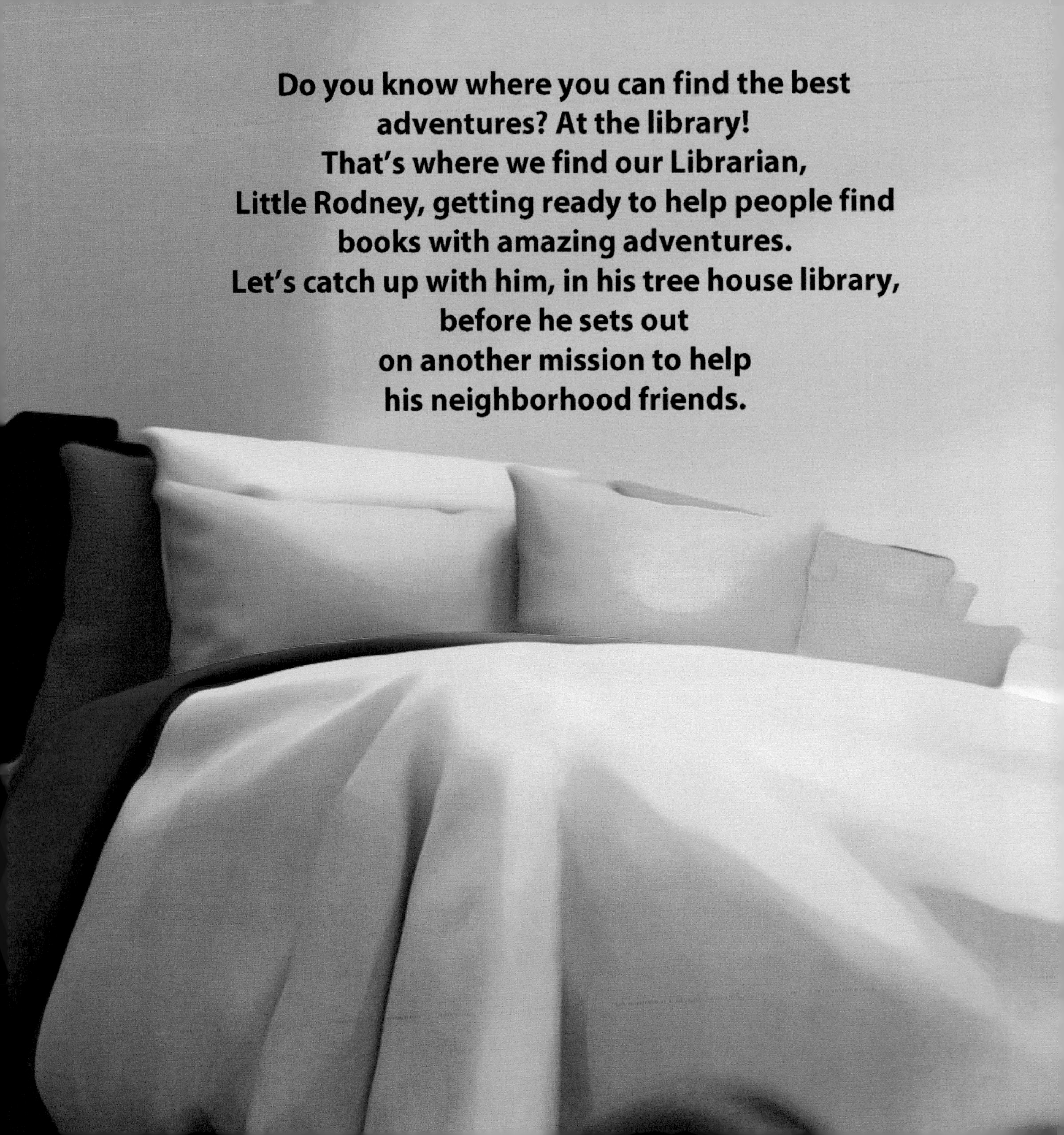

Do you know where you can find the best adventures? At the library!
That's where we find our Librarian,
Little Rodney, getting ready to help people find books with amazing adventures.
Let's catch up with him, in his tree house library, before he sets out on another mission to help his neighborhood friends.

"Hey, Little Rodney, can you help me find a book for my little brother?" says Chloe.

"Step into my office," says Little Rodney.

"Ok, Chloe, we're going to ask you a couple
of questions to see what book
your brother needs."

"That's fine with me," Chloe responds.

"What information is he looking for?"
Little Rodney asks.

"Something about outdoor bugs that eat paper."

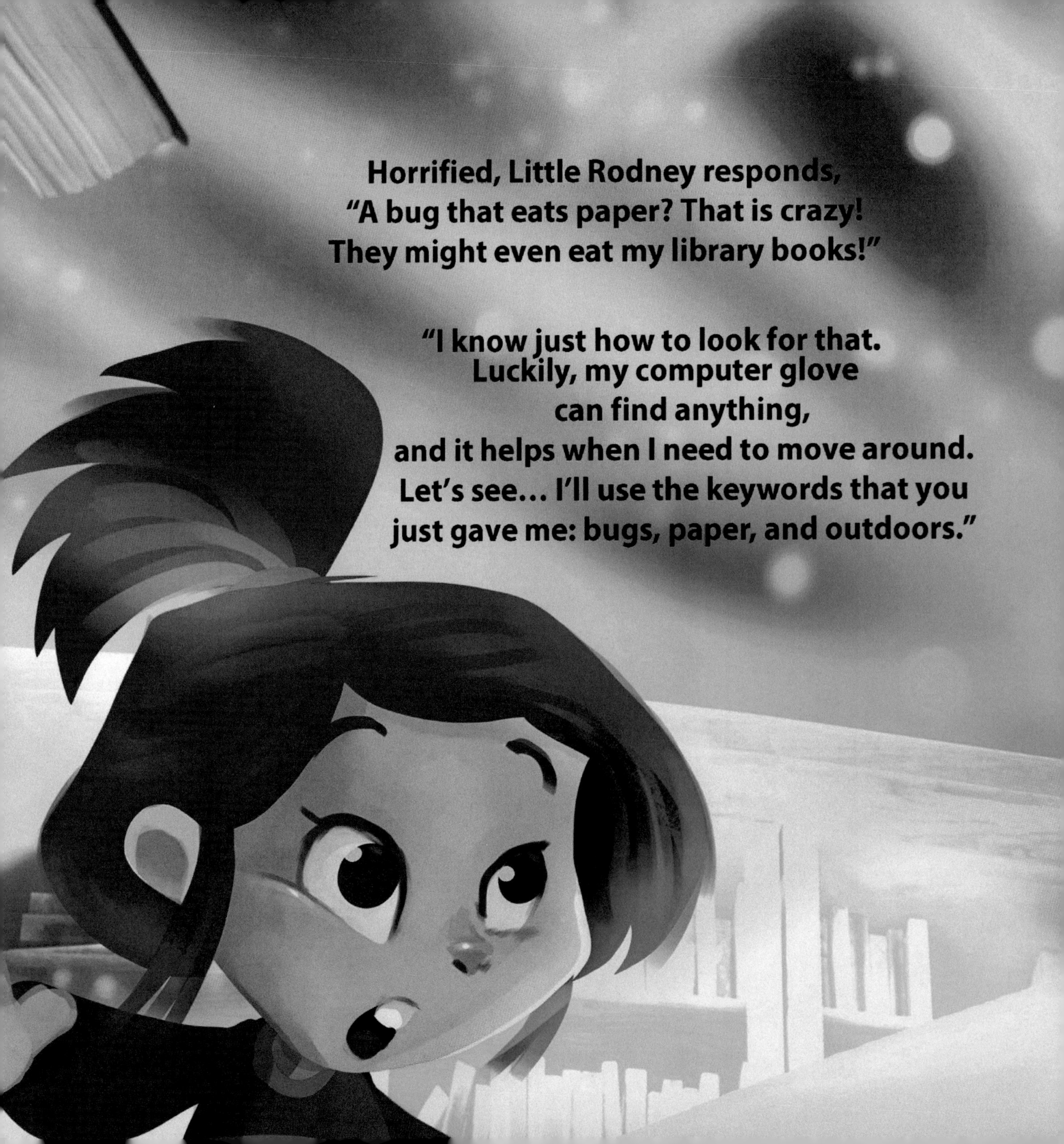

Horrified, Little Rodney responds,
"A bug that eats paper? That is crazy!
They might even eat my library books!"

"I know just how to look for that.
Luckily, my computer glove
can find anything,
and it helps when I need to move around.
Let's see… I'll use the keywords that you
just gave me: bugs, paper, and outdoors."

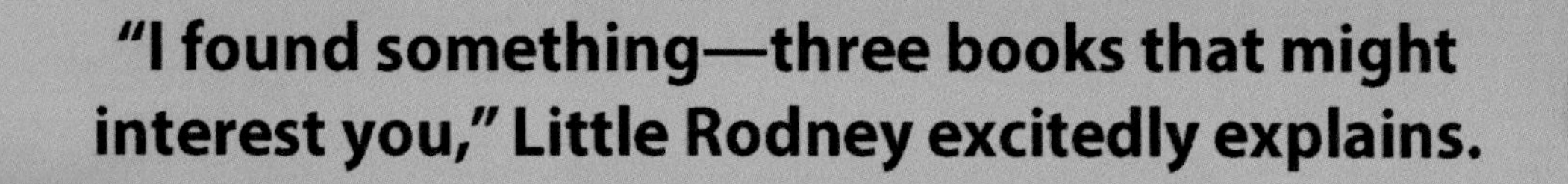

"I found something—three books that might interest you," Little Rodney excitedly explains.

"Let's take a trip to find out which one you want to check out. Step into my office," Little Rodney says, laughing.

"Please take a seat and buckle up," Little Rodney says with a big grin.

"Alright, I'm ready!" Chloe shouts.

The reference desk magically transforms
and drops into the middle of the tree where they
are immediately transported into the first book
world. Little Rodney activates TP Verso,
the computer that helps them find
their way through each book.

"Hello, Little Rodney, I see you're on another one of your adventures for the library," TP says in a courteous voice.

"And who do we have with you today?" asks TP.

"This is my friend Chloe and she would like to check out one of these books. How can we check one out?" Little Rodney asks.

"Miss Chloe will have to find the name of the author, the book's subject, and the call number," TP explains.

"How am I supposed to find that?" Chloe nervously asks.

"I know just where to look on the title page," Little Rodney reassures Chloe.

"Little Rodney, remember, if you do not find the information in time, you'll be trapped in the book! Oh, since the titles of your books are about bugs eating paper, please make sure you are not eaten by one."

"Little Rodney, my brother needs to finish his project or else he will not be able to go on our family camping trip," says Chloe.

"No problem. We'll get home with a little time to spare. My book navigation map says that we should be coming up on the author's name."

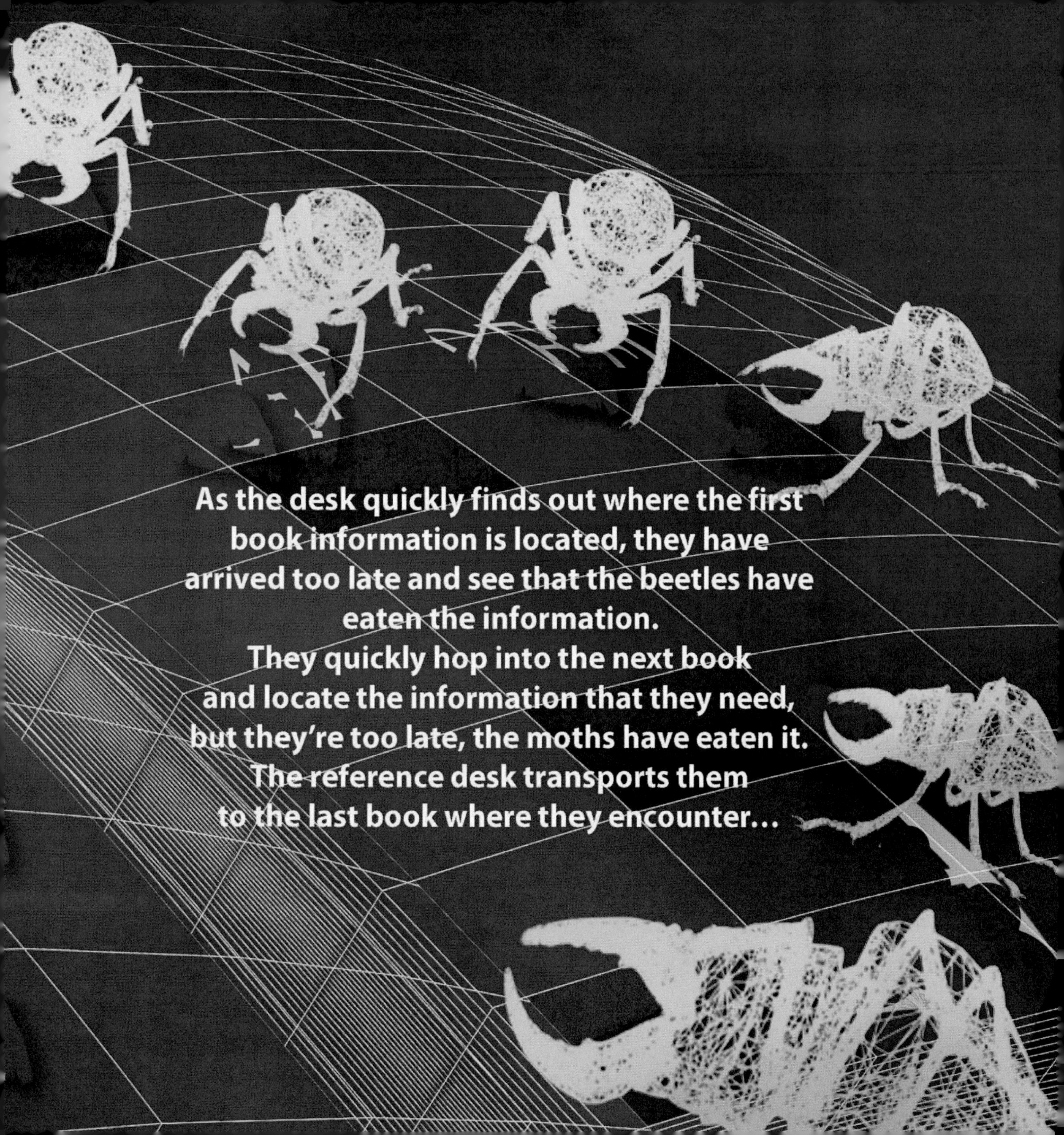
As the desk quickly finds out where the first
book information is located, they have
arrived too late and see that the beetles have
eaten the information.
They quickly hop into the next book
and locate the information that they need,
but they're too late, the moths have eaten it.
The reference desk transports them
to the last book where they encounter…

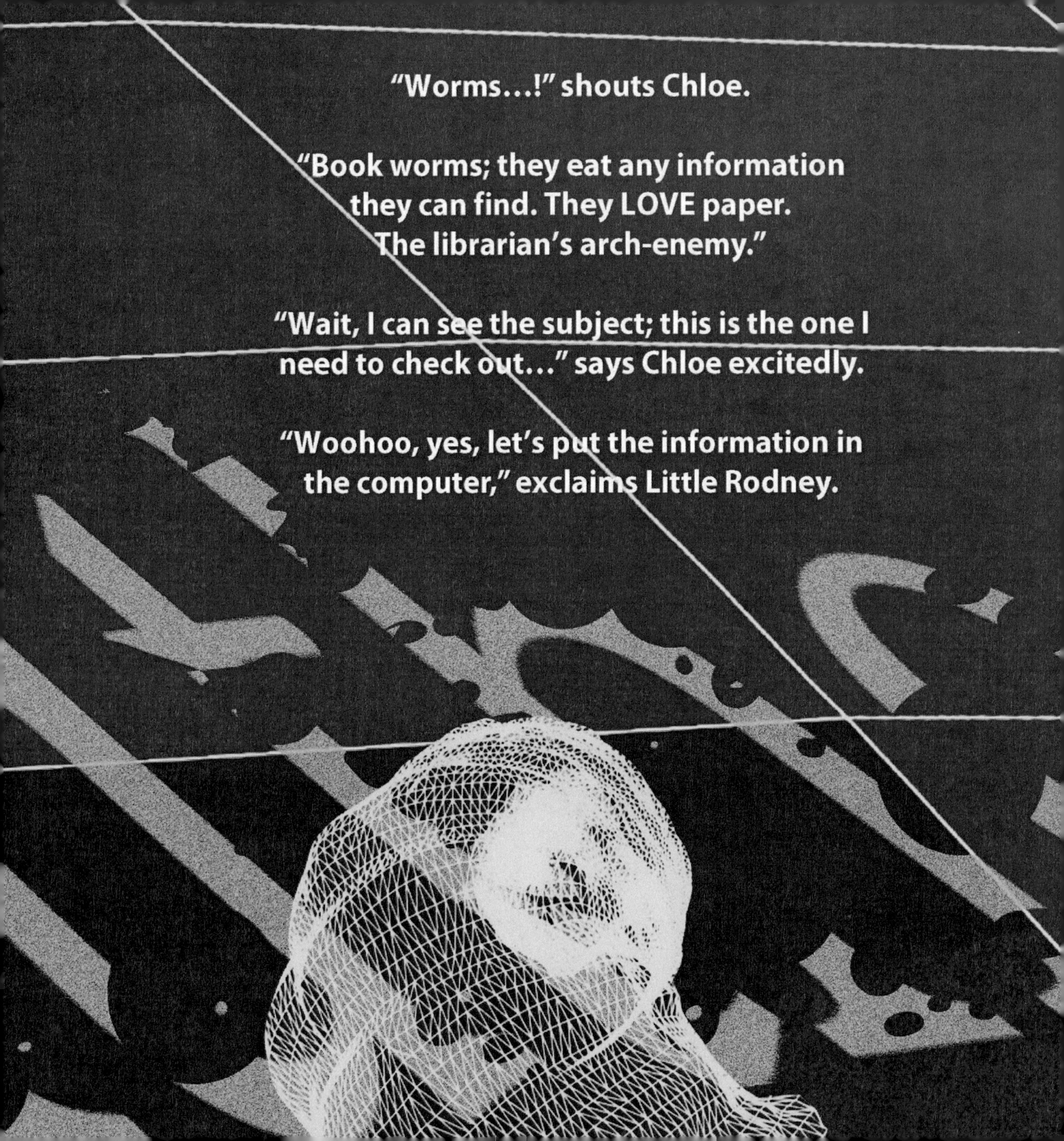

"Worms…!" shouts Chloe.

"Book worms; they eat any information they can find. They LOVE paper. The librarian's arch-enemy."

"Wait, I can see the subject; this is the one I need to check out…" says Chloe excitedly.

"Woohoo, yes, let's put the information in the computer," exclaims Little Rodney.

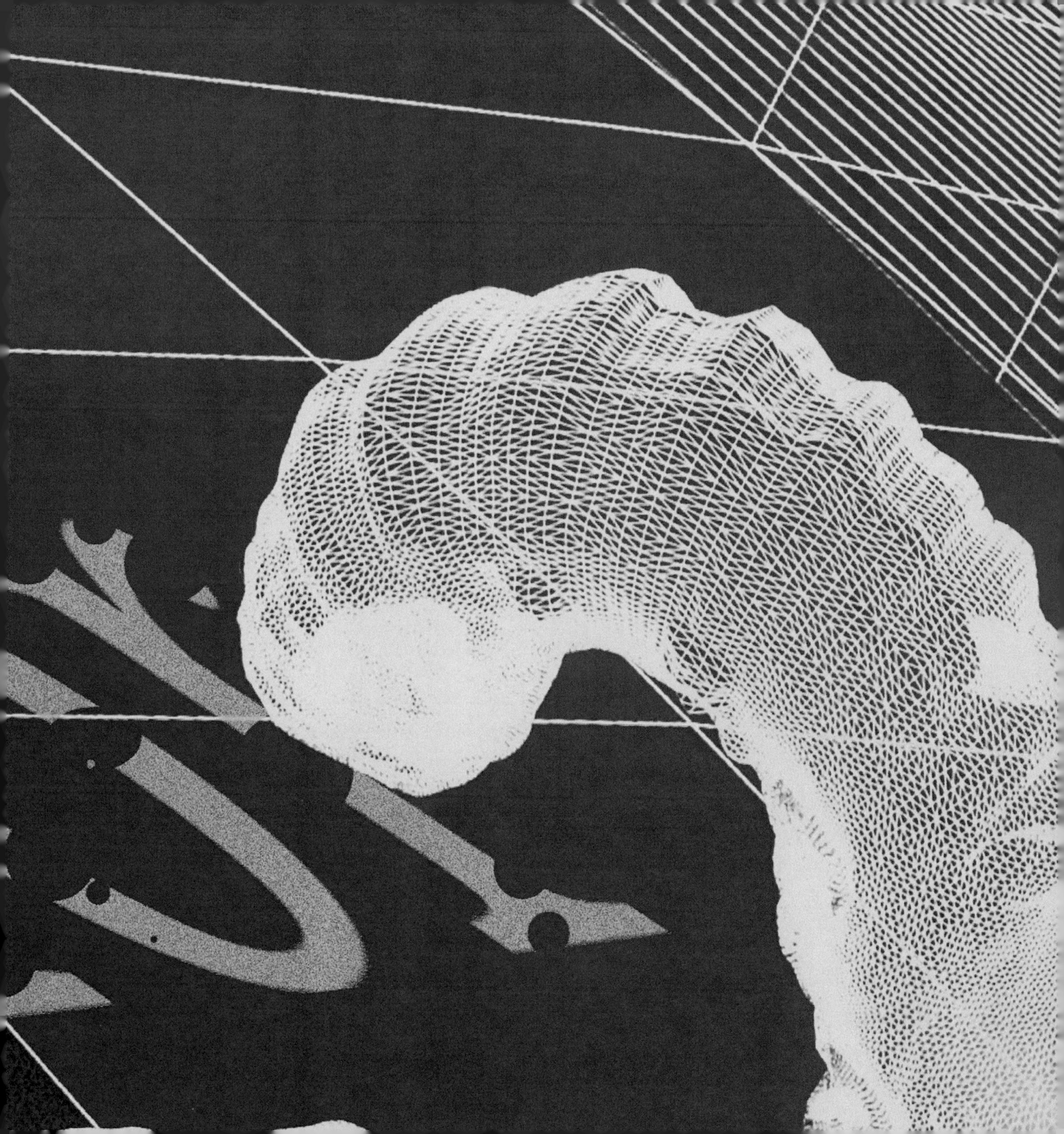

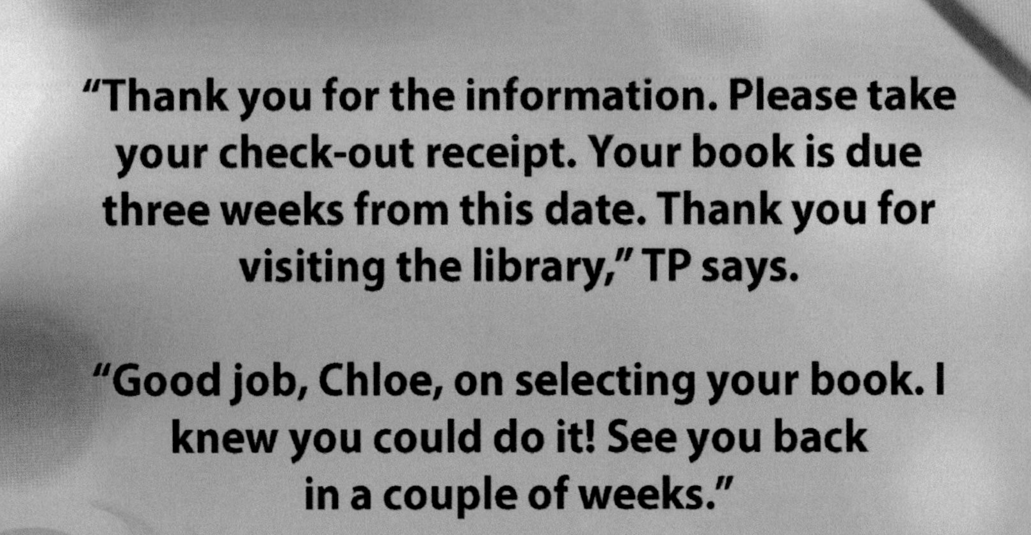

"Thank you for the information. Please take your check-out receipt. Your book is due three weeks from this date. Thank you for visiting the library," TP says.

"Good job, Chloe, on selecting your book. I knew you could do it! See you back in a couple of weeks."

"Bye, Little Rodney.
Thank you," Chloe says.

"Little Rodney, I need your help
to find a book." Jordan says.

Little Rodney gives a big smile
and says, "I can help!"

Made in the USA
Las Vegas, NV
10 March 2023